DISNEP PRESENTS A PIXAR FILM

Cars

Thunder and Lightning

Adapted by Katherine Emmons
Art crafted by Winnie Ho of Disney Publishing's Global Design Group
Inspired by the art and character designs created by Pixar Animation Studios

A Random House PICTUREBACK® Book

Random House 🏠 New York

Library of Congress Control Number: 2005932784
ISBN: 0-7364-2321-4
ISBN-13: 978-0-7364-2321-2

www.randomhouse.com/kids/disney

Printed in the United States of America
10 9 8 7 6 5 4 3 2 1

The day of the big race had finally arrived. One winner would take it all—the Piston Cup trophy and the right to the Dinoco sponsorship! In the quiet of his Rust-eze trailer, a rookie race car prepared himself.

"I'm faster than fast, quicker than quick," he said. "I am Lightning."

He was young. He was fast. He was . . .

. . . Lightning McQueen!

"Ka-chow!" McQueen flashed his lightning bolt sticker as he burst out of his trailer.

The cars in the stands revved their engines for number 95. The hotshot rookie was a true superstar!

But was he fast enough to beat number 43, The King? The King was a real racing legend! In fact, he had won more Piston Cups than any other car in history. After being Dinoco's golden boy for years, The King was ready to retire.

Could he win one last race?

Not if Chick Hicks had his way! Chick had been chasing The King's tail fin his entire career. Now, in The King's final race, Chick was set on becoming the new champion. Engines roared and the ground shook.

They were off!

Right at the start, McQueen zoomed ahead of Chick. Then—
POW!—Chick rammed into McQueen, sending him spinning.
Chick was determined to win, even if he had to use a few
dirty tricks!

As The King took the lead, Chick slammed into another
racer. Behind him, cars screeched and skidded.

Crash! Smash! Crunch! The cars piled up, one after another.

"Get through ***that***, McQueen!" Chick taunted his rookie rival as he looked at the massive wreck he'd created. "A thing of beauty."

Number 86 was one dirty racer!

Coming up from the rear, Lightning McQueen dodged the wreckage. He rode over one car like a skateboard. He leapfrogged another and landed perfectly on the track. What a move! Chick Hicks was not about to stop this rookie! McQueen was at the top of his game.

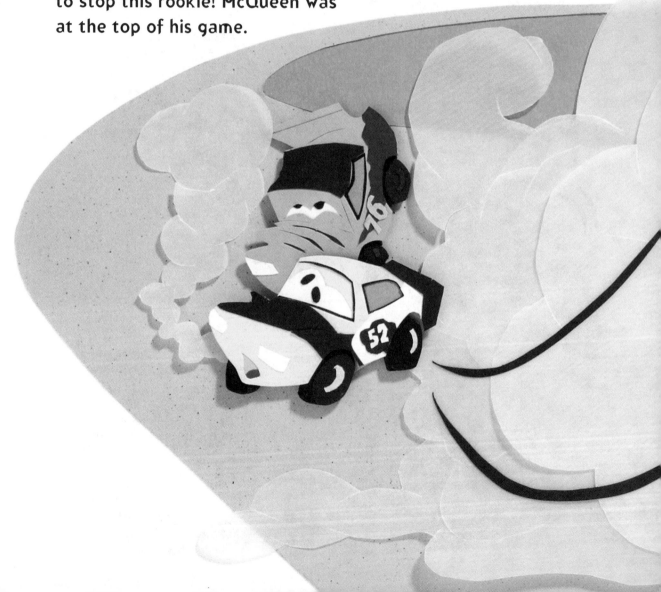

McQueen zoomed past pit row. No pit stops for him. He was a one-man show.

"McQueen made it through!" exclaimed Chick's crew chief. "He's not pitting."

"C'mon! Get me out there!" Chick yelled to his crew.

Eventually, McQueen pulled in for a pit stop. His crew sprang into action.

"No, no, no, no—no tires, just gas!" the rookie insisted. He didn't have time for tires.

"Looks like it's all gas 'n' goes for McQueen today," the announcer said in disbelief as McQueen roared out of the pit. "But it sure is working for him."

Back on the track, the white flag waved. Only one more lap to go!

"Aw, he's got it in the bag!" shouted the announcer. "We're gonna crown us a new champion!"

The fans went wild. McQueen could taste victory, until . . .

. . . ***Ka-blam!***

"Oh, no!" the announcer yelled. "McQueen has blown a tire!"

Only a hundred feet from the finish line, McQueen grunted
and hobbled. He didn't have far to go—he could make it
before Chick and The King caught him. Then . . . **Ka-blam!**
Another tire blew! The rookie was riding on his rims!

Now McQueen was only fifty feet from the finish line, but The King and Chick were gaining on him. Sparks flew as his rear rims scraped the track.

"And down the stretch they come!" shouted the announcer. Chick and The King surged forward as McQueen leaped, hopped, and even stuck out his tongue to get the win by a few extra inches. The checkered flag dropped as the three cars crossed the finish line. It was too close to call!

In Victory Lane, Chick approached McQueen and growled, "The Piston Cup—it's mine, dude. It's mine."

"In your dreams, Thunder," said McQueen.

"What's he talking about—'Thunder'?" asked Chick.

"Hey, you know, because *thunder* always comes after *lightning*," McQueen said with a smile.

The King came over to McQueen. He had some advice for the rookie.

"This ain't a one-man deal, kid," he said.

But McQueen wasn't listening. He had only one thing on his mind: once he was announced as the winner, the Piston Cup and the Dinoco sponsorship would be his.

At last the results were in! Incredibly, all three top cars had finished at once! A tiebreaker race would be held in California in a week.

"Hey, rook! First one to California gets Dinoco all to himself," taunted Chick.

McQueen had a lot to learn, but for now, as he left the Winners' Circle, he thought of one thing: getting to California—and fast. . . . *Ka-chow!*